Eagle Feather Boy Chief

Dallas Ford Lincoln

Disclaimer

This is a work of fiction. Names, characters, places, and incidents either are the product of the author's imagination or are used fictitiously. Any resemblance to actual persons, living or dead, events, or locales is entirely coincidental.

Dedication

To my grandchildren…great and small
and those yet to come.
From your Grandpadallas

Acknowledgments

Lots of folks helped with this story and need to be recognized properly. First I want to again thank my "Canadian Buddy", Martha Henry, for her valuable suggestions and editing skills. And especially to Greg Hetherington for the cover design and Jan A for her layout work. And lastly, thank you grandmanancy, with the "eagle eye". You guys are the best!

Chapter One

An unexpected snowstorm, along with the "white man's disease," forced Eagle Feather's family to move north that winter. The move was planned, but caught the small band of Native Americans off guard and unprepared. A strange new illness had taken its toll on the very young and many of the elders of the tribe. Game was scarce, as most of their hunting ground had been clear-cut by loggers who now occupied the land.

In a futile attempt to provide food to those who still survived, young Eagle Feather fell through the ice on Lake Tamarack. He was rescued by Louise, the mill owner's daughter. Eagle Feather's father was the chief of the tribe and was able to move his little band further north soon after to a place without loggers, and where game was plentiful once again.

The following spring, Eagle Feather found his way back to Lakeville, hoping to reunite with Louise, who was about his age. After a series of adventures that summer, he was invited to live with Louise's family and work at the sawmill alongside her father.

Later that fall, Eagle Feather learned that his father had died and he had now become the tribal chief. Sadly, he bid farewell to Lakeville and those who had taken him in and cared for him. Tears welled up as he struggled with the thought of leaving his friends, "the white ones." Sad, too, as the news of his father's death became almost overwhelming. How could he ever begin to take the place of his father as chief? Filled with fear and dread, he gathered his few belongings and began the long trek north.

Everything in his life had changed. So many had died, including the father he worshiped. The forest where he was born was now reduced to rolling acres of pine stumps as far as the eye could see. He had learned the "white man's" ways and language and now must cast those off along with his adopted "white" family.

Should he stay and abandon the tribe? It would be the easy thing to do. His pace slowed as his thoughts returned to Louise and her parents. He hadn't gone all that far. The sun was still overhead. If he hurried, he could be back to their cabin before dark.

Chapter Two

The sudden death of their chief had caught the little band of Indians completely by surprise. The chief, whose name was Ahmik, which means "beaver," had survived the winter and the "white man's" disease, and was stronger by far than most. When he didn't return from hunting that evening, his wife, Obequa, whose name means "stays at home," was not worried. After all, he was the chief and very brave, and not the least bit afraid to stay in the forest after dark, especially if tracking a wounded dear.

She did worry, though, about their only son, Eagle Feather. Both of his younger sisters had died during the winter, and she herself barely survived this strange illness that had taken so many. How she missed him and wished he would one day return to their lodge. She hated the "white ones" and their ways, and now her only child lived among them. So many moons had passed since he had left them. Obequa had lost track of the number.

To learn her husband had been found dead the next morning was almost more than she could bear. Her only son had left her, her precious daughters had died, and now this! It had to be the coming of the "white ones" causing all this to happen. She cried aloud and cursed the "white devils," while the other women of the tribe tried to comfort her. There was little they could say or do, and most felt like Obequa. For they, too, had lost loved ones to this mysterious disease for which there seemed to be no cure. Now the leader of the tribe was gone. What was to become of them?

Chapter Three

Ahmik was found by one of the older boys who had gotten up early, as this was usually the best time to hunt for game. Ahmik was less than a half mile from the camp, lying face down on a trail that led to a clearing known as the best place to hunt for deer. Not waiting to see if Ahmik was alive or dead, the boy raced back to camp to summon help.

However, Ahmik had suffered a blow to the head and had been dead for quite some time. The tribal members were stunned, as violent death was nearly unheard of in this day and age. Yet, it appeared he had been struck and killed by someone. But why? There were no other tribes in the area, and Ahmik was much respected and a friend to everyone. "Who could have done such a thing?" they asked themselves aloud, searching for some type of explanation.

Left without their beloved leader, gloom and depression began to settle in and the few remaining members of the tribe had to wonder if this was the beginning of the end of their way of life as they knew it. There seemed to be no place they could go that would let them escape from this evil spirit, or whatever it was that was taking its toll on every family. Now the threat of violence had reared its ugly head. It began to appear that the coming of the white man had pushed them to near extinction. Was this to be their fate? Would this generation be the last?

Chapter Four

Bart lugged the dead buck back to his makeshift camp near the clearing in the forest. He would skin the deer first, then check his trap line later in the day. This would be his first taste of meat in days, and he didn't even have to hunt for it. Trapping, not hunting, was his game. Besides, he didn't have any powder or shot for his musket anyway. He chuckled to himself thinking how lucky he had been to come upon that Indian and his fresh kill.

"Stupid savages," he muttered aloud. "Serves him right. They think they own everything and we ain't got no right to none of it. Guess I sure showed that'n. Well, one less to worry about. Bet this here deer hide'll fetch a nice sum. Damn savages, anyway!"

Bart was a loner and somewhat of an outcast in the lumber camps. Best known for cheating at cards, getting drunk, and not paying his debts, his sole source of income was some beaver trappings now and then. Too lazy or drunk to mind his trap lines most of the time, many of the animals he snared died of starvation in the traps, wasting what otherwise would have been fine fur pelts. Bart had a way of just taking what he wanted without regard of the consequences. But bashing an

Indian's head in and stealing his venison? This time Bart had gone too far.

Chapter Five

Eagle Feather picked up his pace and began walking much faster than before. The sun overhead had begun to sink lower on the horizon and he had no idea how far he was from his father's campgrounds. He again thought to return to the sawmill, but just as he turned back, a red-tailed hawk swooped down and lit on a tree branch in front of him. Startled, Eagle Feather retreated as the hawk then flew over his head, away from the direction of the mill, and lit on a branch behind him. The boy attempted once more to make his way towards Lakeville. And once more the hawk flew over his head to interrupt his path, screeching violently. Was this bird trying to tell him something? Was this an omen?

The hawk, screeching as it flew, went further up the path away from the mill, landing on another branch. This time, Eagle Feather began to follow the hawk, and each time he came near, the hawk flew further away until Eagle Feather was actually running to keep up, now going deeper and deeper along the path into the forest. The sun was below the horizon and night was approaching as the scene was repeated over and over again. Finally, when it was too dark to see any longer, Eagle

Feather, exhausted, collapsed beneath the sheltering boughs of a huge pine tree, and fell fast asleep. In a dream that night, he continued to follow the hawk, running and running as fast as he could, but never catching up with this strange bird that continued to urge him on.

When he woke the next morning, somewhat rested, but confused as to his whereabouts, he ate a meager meal of bread and cheese that Louise had wrapped in her handkerchief and had given to him for his journey. Remembering his dream, he began slowly walking in the direction the hawk was leading him the day before. His walk turned into a trot, then a jog, and then he began to run as fast as the wind. He ran until once again he could go no further and sat down to catch his breath.

Nearby he heard the sound of flowing water. A spring of pure water was bubbling up out of the ground barely a few feet away. Crawling to the source on hands and knees, he lay down with his face in the cool water and drank until he could hold no more. The towering pines moaned softly overhead and he fell fast asleep among the green leafy ferns on the forest floor.

Chapter Six

Obequa sat alone in the lodge that now seemed so dark and cold. She needed to get the fire going again. The day old venison stew was cold and should be warmed. She hadn't eaten since the news of her husband's death, and had little or no appetite. How she longed for her son to come home to her and take his father's place as chief of the tribe. It was several days ago that she sent a runner to the mill to tell him of the news in hopes he would do the right thing and come back where he truly belonged.

It was the custom with the tribe for a father to pass the honor of tribal leader down to his eldest son. Without a son, the elders would decide the next chief. Obequa knew that the elders would not like the idea of Eagle Feather becoming their leader, as he had turned to the white man's ways, and seemingly against his own people. A meeting was held to discuss the matter and all had agreed to wait a few days to see if Eagle Feather would return. If he did, then there was little that they could do but to let him take his rightful place as their chief. If not, they would choose a successor among those able to serve. Most felt he would likely never return, choosing instead to become "one of them."

However, out of respect for their departed chief, they would wait.

Chapter Seven

After skinning the deer, Bart decided the trap line could wait a day or two, and he headed instead down to the mill to see what he could trade for the hide. He still owed a bill at the general store and made a mental note not to go there. He had not gone far when he met an Indian boy running in the opposite direction. The hide Bart carried was heavy and the sun was high, making the journey seem longer. Perhaps he could persuade this "young savage" to go back with him and help carry the load.

Eagle Feather recognized Bart as they passed and, knowing his reputation around the mill, continued on without stopping or replying to his asking for help. Bart scowled and gestured obscenely as the boy obviously tried to ignore him and ran past.

"Run away from me then, Injun. You redskins are all alike," Bart called after Eagle Feather. "Ya think ya own everything, including this here path. Next time I see ya, you'll get yours!" he yelled, shaking his fist in the air.

Eagle Feather heard and understood the threat, but paid no attention and just kept running. Besides, he wanted nothing to do with the likes of this kind of "white man." This one was like so many in the lumber camps who felt that Indians were stupid and beneath them. Not like Louise and her family at the sawmill. Eagle Feather would be glad when the loggers were all gone. Apparently, no one could stop them from taking all the timber, leaving nothing behind but acres and acres of tree stumps. So be it, but why did they have to take it all?

Chapter Eight

The path through the pine forest that Eagle Feather followed seemed endless, yet he sensed he was headed in the right direction. He had eaten little since his journey began, and his energy level was low, as were his spirits. He had not seen his father in many moons, and now he was gone forever! The thought of this loss depressed him even further.

Trudging on at a much slower pace, he discovered that the path now branched off in two directions. Both paths appeared to be equally traveled. He closed his eyes and stood quietly waiting, for surely there would come an omen or some type of signal to guide him.

Then he heard a noise. Looking to his left, he spotted a magnificent buck standing in the middle of the path looking directly at him. Could this be the sign he had hoped for?

His spirits lifted and he started to walk towards the deer that suddenly bolted and disappeared, bounding into the thick brush at the side of the trail. At the same moment came the screeching sound of the red-tailed hawk who came out of nowhere, swooping low over Eagle Feather's head and flew straight down the path to the right. Evidently, the hawk had been with him all along and was now showing him the way he must go.

Chapter Nine

The tribal elders decided that they had waited long enough and a new leader must be chosen among those willing to serve. More than one had indicated their desire to become chief, though in fact, few had leadership qualities necessary to become the tribal head. Obequa was notified of their decision, and that a council would be held that evening to choose Ahmik's successor.

Obequa pleaded with them to wait another day or two. In her mother's heart she knew her son would come back to them and take his place as their rightful leader. She begged them to put aside their decision making, and told them that in a dream the night before, a hawk had appeared to assure her that Eagle Feather would return to them before the sun had set three times. Obequa was known to have unusual powers and could sometimes see into the future, so after much discussion, the elders agreed to wait until the sun had set the following day, but no longer.

Word of the council meeting to take place spread quickly among the young and old alike. There had been so much sadness with the death of Ahmik, this would be cause for celebration. Most had hoped that Eagle

Feather would come back to them, but now this did not seem likely. Small groups began to form and speculate as to who would lead them if he did not return. In any event, there would be feasting and celebrating which, it was hoped, would help drive away their sadness.

Chapter Ten

Bart reached the logging camp known as Lakeville late in the afternoon. He was hungry and thirsty after lugging the deer hide all day and headed for the large tented structure down by the sawmill that served as a tavern. Later, when the lumberjacks finished their day's work, the place would be crowded and noisy. This time of day, however, it was quiet except for several old timers playing cards over by the wood stove in the corner. Bart threw the deer hide down on the rough sawn plank that served as a bar and ordered a drink.

"Where'd ya git the hide?" asked the bartender. "Looks like a nice one."

"You might say I got it with the help of one of them injuns up north of here. Might be willing to trade for a little cash and some whiskey."

"We had a runner from that Indian camp come through here a couple of days ago telling the folks at the sawmill that the chief up there had died. Know anything about that?"

"Do tell," Bart said with a knowing smile. "Well, one less of those good for nothin's to worry about, huh? So, how about it? What's that hide worth to ya?"

"Ya know, Bart, you need to change your attitude a bit. Those Indians aren't a threat to us. Maybe we're a threat to their way of life. Did ya ever think about that?"

"I could care less. Now, are ya gonna trade for this here hide or not?"

Bart accepted the bartender's offer of two dollars and a pint of whiskey, finished another drink and left. The bartender just shook his head in disgust and was glad to see him leave. There were always a few bad apples around the camps, but Bart was considered one of the worst.

Chapter Eleven

A ceremonial fire blazed brightly in the center of the camp, radiating heat and compelling all the young and old alike to gather round to absorb its warmth and begin the council that would choose the next chief. There was much anxious chattering and gesturing as the rumor had spread all day that the decision had been made secretly and a new chief would be announced that evening. Since Eagle Feather had not returned to claim his place as chief of the tribe, it befell Obequa, as wife of their fallen chief, to give her formal consent to proceed with the selection of a new leader. Some stood, others sat cross-legged. Several small children ran about squealing and laughing, much to the disgust of the elders as they waited for Obequa to appear.

Obequa had waited all day, praying that Eagle Feather would appear, but now that darkness had fallen, it was apparent that he would not. Dressed in her finest fringed doeskins, she slowly approached the gathering.

As those assembled became aware of her presence, all talking and laughing ceased. With all the dignity afforded the wife of a chief, she entered the circle of those seated near the fire. Only the sound of the crackling flames could now he heard. The wind, as if commanded, became still and the smoke from the fire rose straight into the air above the clearing.

Holding her arms out to all as a silent greeting and, with her eyes focused on the ascending smoke from the fire, she appeared to be asking the Great Spirit for guidance. It was not a woman's place to address the tribal council, but Obequa knew what she must now say. Her speech was slow and could barely be heard, but somehow she managed to thank the elders for their patience in waiting for Eagle Feather to return and acknowledged their right to proceed with the election of a replacement for Ahmik.

With her head held high, she retreated from the circle and, with much dignity, walked slowly back to her lodge alone. In her heart she knew none of those present could replace Ahmik and her only son as leaders.

"Oh, Eagle Feather, my son," she sighed aloud. "Why have you forgotten your people?"

From the council fire came shouting and cheering and she knew that the name of the new leader had been announced.

Chapter Twelve

Eagle Feather continued to follow the seemingly unending path that was leading him ever further away from his adopted family. Still, he continued on, knowing that he must now find his mother and provide for her. What would become of her and the rest of the tribe without his father's guidance? At the moment, his concern for Obequa and the welfare of the tribe was uppermost in his mind.

Sensing that he must be getting close to the camp, he quickened his pace. The path became wider and more traveled and he could see signs that led him to believe he was nearing the end of his journey. Stropping to catch his breath, he noticed a faint wisp of wood smoke slowly rising over the top of the pine trees near a clearing just ahead. He could hear no sounds, but this must be the camp of his father.

His heart was pounding with anticipation, as he found his way across the clearing to a place where the smoke appeared to be coming from. Yet, there were no sounds or lodges anywhere.

What he discovered were the remains of a smoldering campfire and a makeshift lean-to shelter. A partially skinned venison hung from a tree branch nearby. Beneath the skinned animal lay an arrow with the distinct markings of his tribe. Scattered about were some rusty metal traps and the skeletal remains of what appeared to be beaver or something similar. Near the shelter he found an old war club covered with blood. The place was obviously deserted.

By chance, Eagle Feather had stumbled into Bart's pitiful campsite. Finding the arrow from his tribe and the sight of the bloody war club concerned him greatly. He knew he must hurry on, but which way should he go?

The familiar shriek of the red-tailed hawk drew his attention and once again he began to follow the flight of his feathered companion.

Chapter Thirteen

About half an hour later, Eagle Feather thought he could hear sounds off in the distance. He stopped and listened intently. There it was again! Could it be drums he was hearing? It was the sound of drums, but from which direction? Eagle Feather climbed the nearest tree, startling a red squirrel that leapt to the ground dropping the pine cone he had been nibbling.

From his vantage point high above the forest floor, he was able to determine where the sound was coming from. Off on the near north horizon was what appeared to be the red glow of a large fire. Surely, this must be his father's camp. Perhaps he was at last nearing the end of his journey! Quickly, he climbed down from the tree as the red-tailed hawk swooped in low over his head and flew down the path and into the fading light.

The sound of the drumming became increasingly louder and a large plume of smoke rising above the tree line was clearly visible as Eagle Feather pressed on in the direction his winged companion had shown him. Less than a half mile later, he walked unnoticed into the camp of his father.

By now everyone in the camp had gathered around the roaring fire in the ceremonial place reserved for this type of event. Everyone, that was, except Eagle Feather's mother, who had chosen to remain in her lodge. Several of the elders sat together wrapped in colorful blankets. The drumming and chanting continued as many of the younger men danced about the smoke and flames in anticipation of the announcement of the new chief.

Obequa, who had wanted no part of the celebration, finally decided that it would be disrespectful on her part not to attend the ceremony. She was not a mean spirited person. She began slowly walking towards the others gathered about the fire.

Something caught her eye. It was a lone figure walking into the campsite. She brushed away the tears from her eyes as she realized who it was. Unseen by the others, and without a word being spoken, the two solitary figures met and embraced. The full moon, once hidden behind the clouds, suddenly reappeared, shining down on them as if to highlight their reunion.

Chapter 14

The drumming became much louder and the dancing more frenzied then...abruptly stopped! All chanting and talking ceased as the elders stood, each holding out their arms indicating to those assembled that the time had come. A hush fell over the celebrants and all was still, save the snapping and crackling of the fire.

Everyone stood as one of the elders stepped closer to the fire. He spoke in a loud, clear voice, telling them that a new chief had been chosen. He assured them that their dear leader, Ahmik, had guided them in the direction and asked them to remember him at this moment. Now it was time to introduce the new...

Just at that moment, the red-tailed hawk flew into the circle, causing the elder who was speaking to duck instinctively to avoid being hit. Before he could continue with the announcement, there came a stirring and the crowd began to murmur. All heads turned and the crowd parted. Walking arm in arm, Eagle Feather and his mother came into the fire light. Breaking the stunned silence, Obequa spoke.

"My people. The Great Spirit has this day given me my son and you a new chief." Turning to Eagle Feather, she continued, "Your father would be very proud of you today. You have been returned to all of us as our new leader and chief." Obequa stepped away, leaving Eagle Feather standing alone as the red-tailed hawk sailed in and landed on his shoulder.

At first there was nothing but silence. The elders were shocked and simply looked at each other, but no one spoke. Then, one by one the younger men began to move forward, grasping Eagle Feather's hands offering congratulations. Soon everyone followed this gesture and the drumming and celebrating began once again. It was an event that would never be forgotten and would be retold at campfires for many years.

Of course, the elder who had been chosen, but whose name was never announced, was greatly disappointed. However, all the elders accepted Eagle Feather's unexpected return as an omen of good things yet to come. Perhaps the one person who was shocked and affected by all that had happened was Eagle Feather himself. All he ever wanted was to help his mother and his people.

Eagle Feather, now the tribal chief after only fifteen summers, must now become their leader. How do you learn to become a leader after only fifteen summers? Who teaches you the way of the chief? Oh, how he longed for his father's counsel and advice at this very moment!

Chapter Fifteen

For the next several days, Eagle Feather slept in his mother's lodge, waking only to eat, and then falling back into a relaxed sleep, content with just being reunited with her – not caring about his duties as chief. When he was finally rested, his mother tearfully told him about the loss of his two sisters to illness, followed by the murder of his father. Eagle Feather promised her his father's death would be avenged somehow or someway, no matter how long it took.

In the days that followed, Eagle Feather spent his time meeting with the elders and hunting for game. Winter was fast approaching and much venison would be needed to be cured and dried should this year prove to be long and unusually harsh. Each day would now be devoted to finding game and Eagle Feather's skills in finding game were not lacking. Despite the fact that he had not hunted with his bow for over a year, he proved to be the best hunter of all the men in the tribe.

Early one morning, just as the mist was rising from the pond near a clearing not far from his camp, Eagle Feather spotted a magnificently antlered buck, the largest he had ever seen. Without knowing it, he was in the exact spot where his father had been hunting the morning he was murdered.

As the deer bent to drink from the pond, Eagle Feather silently drew his bow and let fly an arrow. The buck reared up on its hind legs, then suddenly bolted into the dense underbrush as though uninjured. Eagle Feather was amazed that he seemed to have missed his target, but decided to go to the spot at the pond's edge where the deer had been standing.

Looking about for the telltale signs of blood, he spotted his arrow lying just beyond, in the weeds. His aim had been true, for there was evidence of blood on the arrowhead. Walking in the direction that the buck had taken in retreat, he noticed more blood on the weeds and leaves. It was now only a question of how badly the animal was injured. If the arrow had hit a vital organ, the deer would not be far. But, if the arrow had merely nicked the hide, the prized stag would be far away by now. A few steps more into the woods would likely settle the issue, and the young hunter's search continued.

Eagle Feather's aim was true and the arrow had passed straight through the area of the heart and lungs. Running for an unbelievable distance after it was struck, the deer fell, mortally wounded, just at the edge of Bart's miserable, but no longer deserted campsite.

Chapter Sixteen

Bart had recently returned to his camp, deciding it was time to check his trap lines. The two dollars he had received for the deer hide was gone, having been spent on liquor and gambling at cards. With his debt unpaid at the general store, he would need fur hides to trade for powder, shot, and provisions for the winter. His search was fruitless. He had forgotten where many traps had been placed and found the rest to be empty. Disgustedly, with nothing to eat in the camp, he finished the last of his whiskey and fell fast asleep in a drunken stupor.

The following morning he was awakened by what he thought was someone coming through the brush. He reached for his rifle, then remembered that it was unloaded. His only other weapon was his skinning knife, but he couldn't remember where he had put it.

Hearing no other sounds, he slowly crept out of his lean-to shelter. Looking about the camp, he neither saw nor heard anything, save the shrill cry of a red-tailed hawk perched on a tree branch near the edge of the campsite. Was there a wildcat or a bear lurking about? Locating his skinning knife, he began slowly walking around the camp's perimeter. The hawk cried out again, drawing his attention. Then he spotted it. Just below the hawk's perch lay a dead or dying deer. This might just turn out to be his lucky day, thanks to the hawk.

Uncertain as to whether the deer was alive or dead, he gave the fallen animal a kick with the toe of his boot, then jumped back. After determining that the animal was indeed dead, he began to look about to see who might have shot and killed it. His first thought was to hide it under some pine boughs lest anyone come looking for their kill.

Judging by the size of the deer, this prize would provide him with food for several months, and the hide would fetch a premium in trade. Hurriedly, he began gathering boughs, chuckling to himself at his good fortune. The hawk overhead cried out again and flew into the woods.

Chapter Seventeen

Eagle Feather had lost the trail of the wounded deer. Perhaps it had not been hit vitally after all. Determined to not let this be a lost cause, he back-tracked to where he had first found specks of blood and then retraced his steps once more. It was no use. He simply found himself back to the same spot where the trail had ended before.

As he stood pondering what to do next, he heard the unmistakable cry of the red-tailed hawk...but from which direction? Silently, he stood listening. There it was again, this time much louder. Pushing his way through the dense underbrush and thorny brambles, he pressed forward in the direction of the hawk's call. Maybe this was a sign that he was on the right path after all.

Bart was aware that someone was coming and moved away from the deer, which he'd partially covered with branches and leaves. Eagle Feather could see the hawk perched on a tree branch just ahead. He pushed and shoved his way through the clumps of bushes and stumbled into the clearing. There stood Bart, poised with his knife in hand, waiting to see who or what was barging into his camp.

Realizing it was just an Indian boy likely looking for the wounded deer, he relaxed, waved his knife and shouted, "What are you doing here? This is my camp! Now git...you...you little savage. You git outta here!"

Eagle Feather recognized this as the place that he had come upon just a few days ago. He also recognized Bart and knew that he would not be welcome. Bart started towards Eagle Feather and menacingly gestured with his knife for him to move away. Eagle Feather began slowly backing up. The hawk flew down, landing on the branch just above his head and cried out once again. Eagle Feather looked up at the sound and stumbled backwards over the hidden deer's carcass. Bart realized Eagle Feather had discovered the hidden deer and began yelling.

"You won't take that deer! It's mine. You damn injuns. Ya thinks ya own everything. Well, not this time ya don't!"

Eagle Feather recovered from his fall and managed to get to his feet. For a moment, he didn't realize what Bart was yelling about, then realized he had fallen over the dead deer. Bart continued across the clearing yelling and motioning for Eagle Feather to go away, but Eagle Feather stood his ground. Obviously, this was the deer that he had taken with is bow. Quickly he notched an arrow to his bow and prepared to defend himself.

Bart was not known for his bravery, in fact, quite the opposite. Bullying children and those smaller than himself was more his style. If it came to a fight, Bart was the first to run. Bart saw Eagle Feather as no match for him in this instance. He continued waving his knife and walking straight towards the young lad, convinced he could simply scare him away.

Eagle Feather was scared alright. Never before had he been threatened with a weapon. Oh, there had been many ugly remarks and taunts about being "an injun," to be sure, but no one had ever harmed him physically. His first reaction was to back away and run, but what would those back at the camp think of their new chief and leader? No, he would not run away like a frightened little boy. Today he would stand his ground like a man.

Chapter Eighteen

Bart was a sloppy man in many ways and often forgot where he set his traps. A lot of this had to do with the fact that he would not tend them for days at a time and, if found to be empty, would frequently move them about.

As he came closer to where Eagle Feather was standing, the red-tailed hawk suddenly shrieked and swooped down from the perch, pecking at Bart's face. Bart swatted at the pesky bird with his knife, but the hawk persisted and continued to fly about his head, beating its wings in his face. Momentarily distracted, Bart changed his course. Instead of heading towards Eagle Feather, he moved sideways to the edge of the clearing as he tried to ward off his attacker.

This was exactly where Bart had placed one of his larger traps in hopes of snaring a wolverine or even a bear. With both arms raised in front of his face, he stepped right on the mechanism that sprung the trap. His cry of anguish must have been heard throughout the forest. The jaws of the trap had broken his leg at the ankle and he was bleeding profusely. Tears ran down his dirty bearded face as he held his broken leg and pleaded with Eagle Feather to help him.

Eagle feather was stunned. At first he didn't realize what had happened and thought this was a ploy to lure him away from the deer. Slowly, with his bow at the ready, he approached his howling attacker and discovered the man was indeed trapped and knew Bart was in serious trouble. Without speaking, Eagle Feather backed away and began to retrace his steps into the woods.

Bart cried out in anguish. "Hey, come back here! I need help. I won't hurt you. Don't leave me. Please, come back!"

Eagle Feather continued on his way, disregarding Bart's pitiful please for help for he knew that it would take at least one or two more braves to get Bart out of the jaws of the huge iron trap. Bart was going to need medical attention as well. Perhaps Obequa could be of help in that regard.

The cries for help became fainter as Eagle Feather began to run as fast as he could back to his camp.

Chapter Nineteen

Even at this pace, it took him nearly thirty minutes to finally reach the camp. Several elders were gathered near the common fire pit, exchanging stories about their hunting experiences that morning. Nearly out of breath, Eagle Feather managed to describe what had just happened, and that help was needed to free the trapped white man and to drag the deer back to camp.

As Eagle Feather continued to describe his encounter with this strange, angry man, the elders surmised who he had met. Bart had recently threatened several members of the tribe, accusing them of stealing the game from his traps. He had warned that he would shoot them if ever he found them hear his traps.

After a lengthy discussion, it was agreed that three of the younger braves should accompany Eagle Feather and his mother back to help Bart. Frankly, they were far more interested in fetching the much needed venison than helping a cantankerous trapper who wasted most of what he killed.

The sun was high overhead and several hours had passed since Bart had stepped into his own trap. Eagle Feather knew that by now Bart would have lost a considerable amount of blood, and encouraged those with him to hurry a little faster. The others, knowing who they were going to help, seemed not quite as concerned, continuing on at a more leisurely pace.

Suddenly, there came a howling sound in the direction of Bart's camp. Eagle Feather held up his hand, halting the procession, and gestured for quiet. There it was again! Not really a human sounding voice...more of an animal cry. The howling grew louder. The shriek of the red-tailed hawk momentarily distracted them as it flew down and landed on a branch just above Eagle Feather's head.

The howling turned to growling sounds as the wide-eyed braves looked at one another, wondering if they should continue in that direction. The hawk let out another shrill cry and flew off towards Bart's camp. Obequa looked sternly at the three young braves and indicated that they were to follow in the same direction. Eagle Feather was already on his way, now at a run, trying to keep up with his red-tailed hawk companion.

Chapter Twenty

Reaching the edge of the clearing where the dead deer lay, Eagle Feather stopped and waited for the others to appear. The scene there was now strangely quiet. The only sound was the wind in the white pine branches high overhead. The deer was still there covered with branches, right where he had found it.

Looking across the clearing, it was apparent that someone or something had torn Bart's shelter to pieces. It was completely destroyed and scattered about. Eagle Feather clutched his bow a little tighter and reached for an arrow. As the others quietly approached, Eagle Feather silently indicated to the three braves that they were to carefully circle the edge of the clearing and that Obequa was to remain where she stood.

Two of the braves with bows ready, went around to the right, while Eagle Feather and the other brave went left. The four circling braves met half way around the cleared campsite. The oldest shrugged his shoulders as they had found nothing nor anyone. Eagle Feather looked to where he had last seen Bart.

Standing there was his mother, the hawk resting above her on a low hanging branch. Silently, she motioned for them to come to her. Still anxious, the four walked over so slowly across the clearing, looking both left and right with their bows notched with arrows. There was no need. Obequa had found Bart's trap and what was left of Bart. Bits of human hair and scraps of clothing were scattered about and blowing in the wind. In the unopened jaws of the trap there remained a bloody boot with what appeared to be a bone sticking out of it.

The four braves were startled at the gruesome sight and shuddered as they anxiously looked about, wondering if they were still in danger. Obequa quietly turned and began walking softly back to the half-hidden deer. The other four with bows drawn, cautiously backed away from the trap, still looking in all directions, fully expecting something to jump out of the woods and attack them.

Chapter Twenty-One

Satisfied that they were no longer in any danger, the four braves located Obequa, who was already in the process of field-dressing the deer, as she had done many times before. Eagle Feather ordered two of the braves to stand guard, and the other one was to find a suitable pole for transporting the deer back to camp. Eagle Feather bent to help his mother and the task was soon completed. The front and hind legs of the deer were tied to a sturdy pole and the trek back to the camp began.

The sun had begun to slip behind the towering pines surrounding the trail and soon they would be safely back at their camp. Red squirrels and small birds could be heard chirping all about them as they hiked on. Tonight there would be fresh venison to share and a tale to tell of Chief Eagle Feather and the hawk. A tale that would be told and retold for years to come.

Suddenly, from out of nowhere came the red-tailed hawk, sweeping low over Eagle Feather's head, circling once. Then, without making a sound, flying up over the trees and disappearing into the twilight.

The End

Dallas Ford Lincoln

Visit Mr. Lincoln's Amazon Author Page for other books:

http://tinyurl.com/p7jnxh3

Big Jim and the Tamarack Queen

https://www.createspace.com/5288788

The Scout Cabin

https://www.createspace.com/5027217

The Pickle Docks

https://www.createspace.com/4985646